Jitters

By
Alison Paroly

Co-creator
April Bates

Illustrated by: Violeta Honasan

To order additional copies of this book, contact:
Xlibris LLC
1-888-795-4274
www.Xlibris.com
Orders@Xlibris.com

I would like to thank my friend, and co-creator April Bates. Thank you for working day in and out with me to bring an idea to life. I would also like to thank my husband Rich, who has supported me and put up with me every step of the way.

It's time! OH MY, It's time!
The alarm wakes me with a **BEEP.**
I pull the covers over my head,
UGH---I really want to sleep.

I **yawn** and **stretch**, I'm out of bed,
I'm famished as can be.
I get dressed, run down the stairs,
eggs and toast for me!

BEEP!

Going through my checklist...
Did I pack all that I need?
My lunch, my bag, my glasses too,
and favorite book to read.

I **DASH** out the door.
I feel like I should hurry.
I'm feeling dizzy, I feel faint---
My vision's getting blurry.

This ride feels like **FOREVER**.
My palms are getting sweaty.
Yikes, I sigh out loud,
I hope that I am ready.

I'm here, Ok I made it.
I'm gazing at the school.
I wonder if the kids in my room,
will think that I am cool?

I picture myself walking,
Into the building standing TALL,
OR...Will I miss the step out front,

S*t*u*m*b*le a*n*d a*l*mo*s*t fa*l*l?

I stroll into the school,
And I'm greeted with a smile.
I have to find the room I'm in.
This might take a while.

Your new room is 123,
Have a great first day!
I begin walking down the hall.
I'm sure I'll find my way.

I'm moving kind of sluggish.
THERE IT IS! I SEE THE DOOR!
I'm feeling weary... I can't make it.
The PRESSURE! Two steps more.

I'm staring at the entrance—
I can't seem to take my eyes away.
I spy the children walking in.
Will they want to stay?

Inhale in---Exhale out,
I pant and gasp, then GO!
One foot in front of the next,
I'm so nervous. Does it show?

I peek my head into the room.
I can see the kids inside.
I'm thinking maybe now is the time—
to bolt away and hide!

I reason with myself,
You can do it, you'll be fine.
You're bold and fearless, brave as can be.
I cross the finish line!

I imagined I would see...
Kids standing on their chairs,
Throwing things around the room,
Spitballs flying through the air.

Making paper airplanes,
Drawing on the desks,
Toys scattered everywhere,
A **huge, colossal mess!**

Hopping, skipping, jumping
Playing tag, running around
Crayons, pencils, rulers
Scattered all over the ground.

Kids perched up on shelves,
Tossing books high in the air.
Arguing about something-silly,
Pointing fingers, pulling hair!

BU

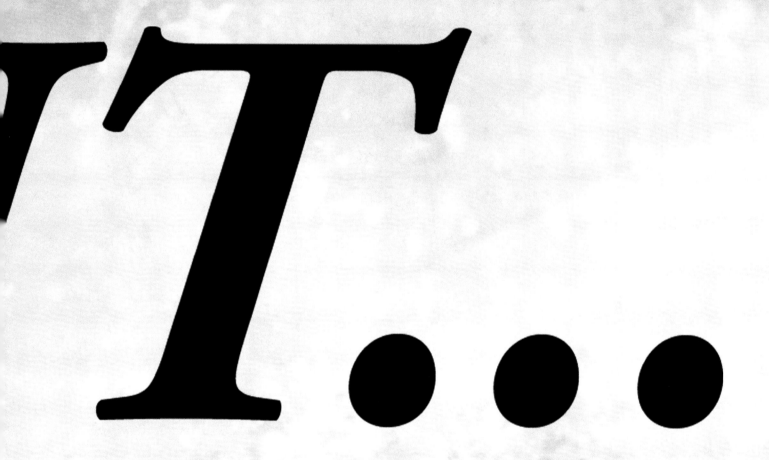

I survey the classroom.
And much to my surprise...
I hear the sounds of laughter,
And **not** the sounds of cries.

The children are strolling around the room,
Conversing, breaking the ice.
The nervous feeling is disappearing!
The class looks very nice.

Perh

aps....

Maybe it's time—
to introduce myself.
I take off my coat,
And place my bag upon the shelf.

Excuse me friends,
I say nice and clear.
I am your teacher,
Welcome to the beginning
of the new school year!

I am so thrilled to meet you.
At the same time, you can see—
Everyone gets nervous.
Everyone, including **me.**

Today is a new beginning for me.
I wonder what this year will bring.
Today, this is how I am feeling...

_____

_____

_____

_____

_____

_____

_____

The year has gone by.
I have so much to say.
These are the feelings,
I'm feeling today...

_____

_____

_____

_____

_____

_____

_____

Reading Essentials® in Science

DIVERSE POPULATIONS

Protists and Fungi

PAUL PISTEK

PERFECTION LEARNING®

Editorial Director: Susan C. Thies
Editor: Mary L. Bush
Design Director: Randy Messer
Book Design: Emily J. Greazel
Cover Design: Michael A. Aspengren

Paul Pistek is an instructor of biological sciences at North Iowa Area Community College.

To my family—Julie, Grace, Lucas, and Seth

Image credits

©CORBIS: p. 6; ©Visuals Unlimited/CORBIS: p. 7; ©Clouds Hill Imaging Ltd./CORBIS:
p. 12 (bottom); ©WSL Handout/Reuters/CORBIS: p. 19; ©Karen Tweedy-Holmes/CORBIS:
p. 23 (top); ©Mediscan/CORBIS p. 27 (top); ©Nick Hawkes; Ecoscene/CORBIS: p. 33;
©Dennis Kunkel/PhototakeUSA: pp. 13, 35; ©Scott Sinklier/Ag Stock: p. 36

©CORBIS Royalty-Free: pp. 3 (bottom), 31; Corel Professional Photos: front cover, pp. 3 (top), 4,
28 (bottom), 32 (top), 37 (bottom); DK: pp. 23 (bottom), 25; iStock International: back cover,
pp. 3 (middle), 5, 10–11, 22 (bottom), 28 (top), 34, 37 (middle), 38; Perfection Learning: pp. 9, 10,
12 (middle), 14, 16, 17, 20, 21, 22 (middle), 27 (bottom); Photos.com: pp. 1, 8, 22 (top), 26, 29, 30,
32 (bottom), 37 (top), 39

For information, contact

Perfection Learning® Corporation
1000 North Second Avenue, P.O. Box 500
Logan, Iowa 51546-0500.   10/09
Phone: 1-800-831-4190   18.95
Fax: 1-800-543-2745
perfectionlearning.com

1 2 3 4 5 6 PP 11 10 09 08 07 06

PB ISBN 0-7891-7039-6
RLB ISBN 0-7569-6647-7

Contents

chapter 1

On the Lookout

You've been hiking through the mountains for several hours. When you spot a creek running alongside the path, you realize how thirsty you are. The water appears clean and pure. Surely a little drink from this clear mountain stream wouldn't be harmful, right? Wrong! Days after drinking the water, you could find yourself with a severe stomachache. The culprit? A microscopic **protist** called *Giardia intestinalis*.

Hiking also gives you an appetite. When you come across some mushrooms under a fallen oak tree, you consider snacking on them. After all, they look just like the ones you had on a pizza a few days ago. However, what you assume are delicious edible mushrooms may, in fact, be poisonous toadstools. The umbrella-shaped **fungi** could make you very sick or even kill you!

Where Are They?

Besides on your mountain hike, where can protists and fungi be found? Almost everywhere! You may have seen them in the form of seaweed at the beach. Or you may have spotted them as a fuzzy growth on old food in your refrigerator. Perhaps you've noticed a musty smell in your basement or bathroom or seen gray or green discoloration on shaded areas of your house or sidewalk. If you've had any of these experiences, then you've had a close encounter with protists and/or fungi.

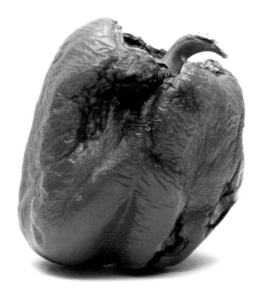

What Are They?

Protists and fungi are diverse groups of organisms. The two groups do, however, have a few things in common.

Both protists and fungi are eukaryotes. This means that all of their cells have a nucleus, or center, where genetic information is stored.

All living things need water to live and grow. Because protists and fungi don't drink water like animals do, they need to live in an environment where water is readily available. Both groups, therefore, generally prefer warm, moist environments.

Both groups are neither plant nor animal. Fungi are members of the Fungi kingdom. This group includes yeasts, molds, and mushrooms. Protists are a collection of different eukaryote organisms that don't belong to either the fungi, plant, or animal kingdom. This group includes protozoans, algae, amoebas, and *Paramecium*.

If You Aren't a Eukaryote, Then What Are You?

Organisms that don't have a nucleus are called *prokaryotes*. Bacteria are prokaryotes.

Tracing the Path of Science

The classification of organisms has existed for thousands of years. The Greek philosopher Aristotle (384–322 B.C.) used a system called "scale of nature" that was based on the complexity of organisms. Simple organisms were placed in lower categories, while more complex ones were higher. It was as if each type of organism had its own rung on a biological ladder.

Carolus Linnaeus

In 1735, a Swedish physician and botanist named Carolus Linnaeus published *Systema Naturae*, a book that described a way to classify and name organisms by their physical characteristics and manner of living. Linnaeus's two-part naming method (genus/species) is still used today and was the basis of what is now known as the branch of biology called *taxonomy*.

Since Linnaeus, the method of classifying organisms has developed into an approach called *systematics*. This process analyzes information about physical, chemical, and genetic similarities and differences among organisms (both living and extinct). The result is a more accurate taxonomic map that not only classifies and names but also describes the history of life, showing how all living organisms are related in one large family tree.

chapter 2

Presenting the Protists

Scientists have been fascinated with protists since scientist Anton van Leeuwenhoek first observed them more than 300 years ago. Currently, about 80,000 species of protists have been identified and named. Scientists believe there may be as many as 600,000 different species of protists in existence. Although they share the name *protist*, these organisms are amazingly varied in form and behavior. **Algae**, diatoms, *Paramecium*, and **amoebas** are examples of protists.

The Future of Protists

In the past, protists were considered members of the Protista kingdom. However, because the group is so diverse and new technology has revealed more information about these organisms, scientists are currently rearranging the group into many new kingdoms.

Chlorophyta (green alga)

Body Basics

Protistan body size can range from less than 5 micrometers to about 60 meters. Protists can consist of one cell (unicellular) or many cells (multicellular). The majority of them are unicellular. Each of these cells has a complex design that enables it to survive. These cellular designs vary among the different species of protists.

Cell walls provide support for many protists and keep them from bursting when they fill with water. Some protists have flexible outer cell walls made of cellulose, which is similar to the cell walls of plants. This is common in many forms of algae, water molds, and slime molds. Other protists form cell walls that are more rigid. For example, foraminiferans produce a chalky outer shell called a *test*. Diatoms, a form of unicellular algae, have yet another type of outer structure. These organisms produce a silica (glassy) covering consisting of two parts that are similar to a hatbox and lid.

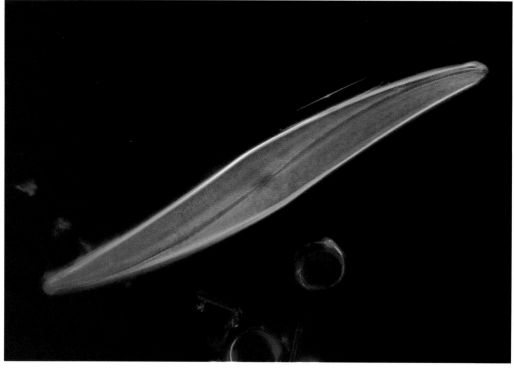

Diatom

Some protists lack a cell wall altogether. In many cases, the cell membrane on these protists is more complex than typical membranes and gets more support from structures inside the cell called *microtubules*. This type of cell membrane is referred to as a pellicle. A pellicle provides strength while still maintaining flexibility.

Many freshwater protists that lack a cell wall rely on an organelle called a *contractile vacuole*. This functions like the sump pump in a basement, pumping excess water out of the cell.

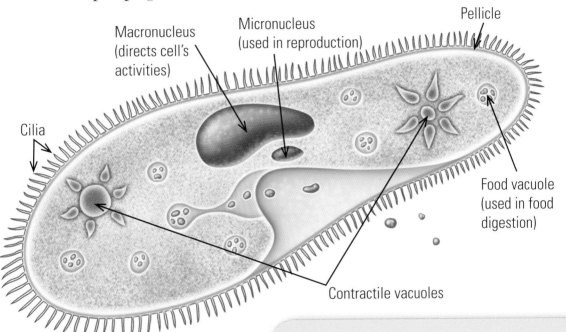

Macronucleus
(directs cell's
activities)

Micronucleus
(used in reproduction)

Pellicle

Cilia

Food vacuole
(used in food
digestion)

Contractile vacuoles

***Paramecium* Structure**

An Extra Wall of Protection

Some protists can form cysts when conditions change. A cyst is a thick-walled resting stage that's resistant to drying out or freezing. Once favorable conditions return, the protist will awaken and become active again.

Locomotion is an important part of daily life for many protists. There are three main ways these organisms get around on their own—by flagella, cilia, or pseudopodia.

Flagella
A flagellum is a long whiplike extension that pushes or pulls a protist along. *Euglena* (you GLEE nuh) are common **flagellates** found in pond water.

Cilia
Cilia are short extensions that are usually present in large numbers. Cilia work together to produce fluid, graceful movement like that of the many oars on a Viking ship. Cilia can also be arranged in a way that allows a protist to scurry along a surface like a centipede across a basement floor. In some cases, cilia are used to move or draw food into a protist. *Paramecium* are **ciliates** commonly found in pond scum.

Pseudopodia
Pseudopodia are flowing extensions that help some protists move. By extending parts of their cells (the pseudopodia), the protists are able to "ooze" in a certain direction. Movement by pseudopodia is also used to help encircle and ingest food. Protists that move this way are often called *amoebas*, even though they don't all belong to the *Amoeba* group.

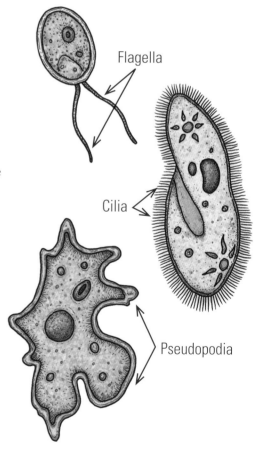

Flagella

Cilia

Pseudopodia

Free Floaters

Plankton are protists that float freely near the surface of water and primarily move with the drifting of the currents. Many forms of algae, including seaweeds, are plankton.

Time to Eat!

The way protists acquire nutrients is as varied as the protists themselves. All protists, however, fit into one of three categories—producers, consumers, or decomposers.

Producers

Producers are organisms that can generate their own nutrients using inorganic (nonliving) materials such as minerals and water. Because they use photosynthesis to do this, they are often called **photoautotrophs**. The word *algae* is an informal term often used to define the plantlike group of protists that carry out photosynthesis. Algae have a variety of body forms, and their color depends on the presence of different pigments. Dinoflagellates, diatoms, golden algae, brown algae, red algae, green algae, and many *Euglena* are all considered algae.

A Side Note on Seaweed

Large multicellular marine algae are often called *seaweed*. The largest seaweeds are from the brown algae group and are known as kelp.

11

Consumers

Consumers are organisms that must attain energy from other living things. They are also known as **heterotrophs** because they rely on other organisms or their by-products for nutrients. Because this group resembles animals (consumers that are able to move on their own), they are informally known as **protozoans**.

Protozoans take in nutrients through one of two main ways—absorption or **endocytosis**. Absorption occurs when small organic molecules are transported through the cell membrane. Endocytosis is the process in which a membrane engulfs food and takes it into the cell. When protozoans use endocytosis to consume large items like entire cells, the process is referred to as **phagocytosis**. Amoebas and ciliates feed in this manner.

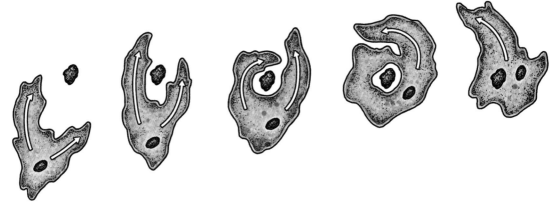

Amoeba Phagocytosis

Mixed-Up Euglena

Euglena can actually be both producers and consumers. When sunlight is available, *Euglena* rely on photosynthesis. When sunlight is lacking or limited, these protists can absorb organic nutrients from their surroundings. Because of this dual ability, *Euglena* are called *mixotrophs*.

Decomposers

A decomposer is a special kind of heterotroph that feeds on nonliving organic matter. Decomposers are considered recyclers because they break down organic matter into its basic inorganic parts. This allows producers to use the materials again and continue the cycle of life. Water molds and slime molds are protistan decomposers.

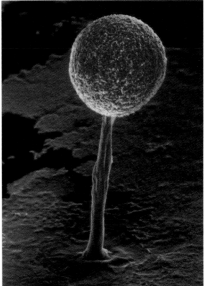

Slime mold

Protistan Lifestyles

Most protists are considered free-living, meaning they live independently of others. There are some protists, however, that live with others. This type of lifestyle is called **symbiosis**. An organism that lives on or in a larger organism is usually called the *symbiont*. The larger organism is called the *host*. Symbiosis comes in three main forms—mutualism, commensalism, and parasitism. All three of these forms are represented in protists.

Mutualism

Mutualism is a relationship in which both the symbiont and the host benefit. An example are flagellated protists called *trichonymphs*. Trichonymphs live in the guts of termites, engulfing and digesting the wood that's eaten by the insects. The simple sugars released by the digestion process are used by both the trichonymphs and the termites.

Commensalism

Commensalism is a relationship in which one partner benefits but the other is neither helped nor harmed. An example would be the green algae that live on the bark of trees. The algae have a place to live and grow, and the trees are neither helped nor hurt by the presence of the algae.

13

Parasitism

Parasitism is a relationship in which the parasite (symbiont) benefits at the cost of its host. These benefits usually come in the form of nutrients and/or a home for the parasite. Some types of algae, protozoans, and molds enjoy parasitic relationships. In some cases of protistan parasitism, there may be more than one host. *Plasmodium* is a parasite that causes the disease malaria in human hosts. These protists use mosquitoes as a host as well. The mosquitoes can then infect humans with the disease.

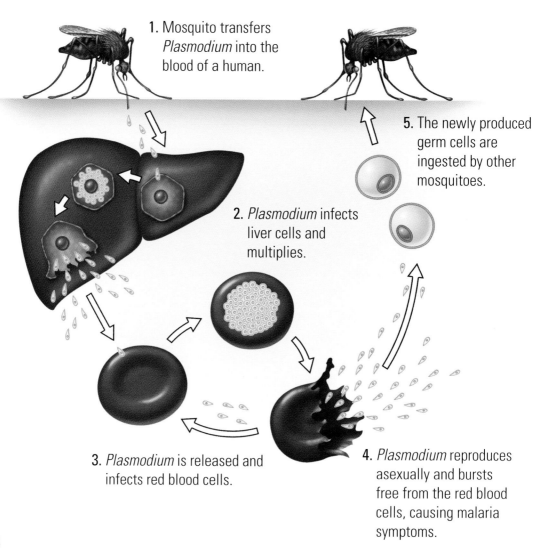

1. Mosquito transfers *Plasmodium* into the blood of a human.

2. *Plasmodium* infects liver cells and multiplies.

3. *Plasmodium* is released and infects red blood cells.

4. *Plasmodium* reproduces asexually and bursts free from the red blood cells, causing malaria symptoms.

5. The newly produced germ cells are ingested by other mosquitoes.

Home Is Where the Habitat Is

Protists thrive in freshwater and saltwater environments. They can be found anywhere in the water. Some may float on the top, while others are anchored to a surface deep underwater.

Many protists can take advantage of life on land as well—as long as there is a source of water nearby. Many protozoans and molds and some types of algae live in or on terrestrial organisms, getting their moisture from the host. Other protists reside in soil or under organic debris, where moisture is retained. In places where the climate is extreme, some protists have learned to respond quickly when conditions are right, taking in the moisture and nutrients they need. When conditions turn hostile again, these protists will either enclose themselves in a protective cyst or will rely on their **dormant**, weather-resistant offspring to continue the cycle of life the next time conditions are favorable.

Watermelon Snow

In some cases, protists have adapted so they are able to stay active even during extreme conditions. The green alga *Chlamydomonas nivalis* is known to create an effect known as "watermelon snow." The algae's dense pink algal blooms are often seen high on snowfields and glaciers in the Sierra Nevada. This occurs during summer months when temperatures are still subfreezing. The pink color is due to a red pigment that's present in the algae. This pigment is believed to protect the delicate protist cells from extreme solar radiation while at the same time absorbing heat to warm the cells and their surroundings.

The Cycle of Life

Protistan life cycles are as varied as the group. In some cases, the process is very simple. In other cases, the process has many stages. Some protists reproduce either sexually or asexually, while others reproduce using both methods. Asexual reproduction results in the formation of offspring that are genetically identical to the parent. Sexual reproduction is the result of two cells joining to form offspring that are genetically different from the parent or parents.

Asexual Reproduction

Binary fission is a form of asexual reproduction that occurs when a unicellular organism divides to form two identical daughter cells. Most protozoans reproduce through binary fission.

Sexual Reproduction

Zygote formation is the result of sexual reproduction. A zygote is formed when two sex cells called *gametes* and their nuclei fuse together to form one functional cell. This cell then develops into an offspring. Algae and water molds reproduce through zygote formation.

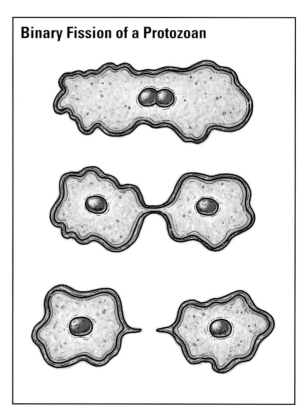

Binary Fission of a Protozoan

Life Cycle of *Ulva* (Large Marine Green Alga)

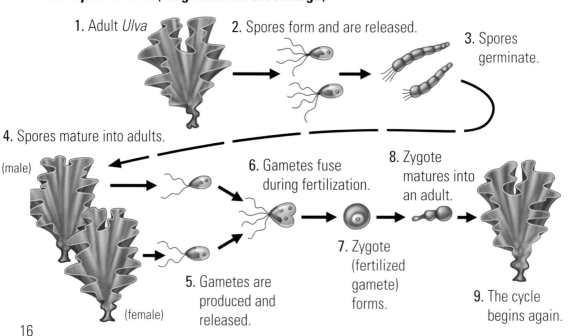

1. Adult *Ulva*
2. Spores form and are released.
3. Spores germinate.
4. Spores mature into adults.
   (male)
5. Gametes are produced and released.
   (female)
6. Gametes fuse during fertilization.
7. Zygote (fertilized gamete) forms.
8. Zygote matures into an adult.
9. The cycle begins again.

Conjugation is a sexual process seen in ciliates. Ciliates have two types of nuclei. One nucleus, called the *micronucleus*, is used primarily for the process of reproduction. The other nucleus, called the *macronucleus*, is responsible for directing all the daily activities of the cell. During conjugation, the micronuclei between two compatible cells are exchanged. Following conjugation, each ciliate normally completes reproduction by dividing to form four daughter cells. *Paramecium* reproduce by conjugation.

Paramecium Conjugation

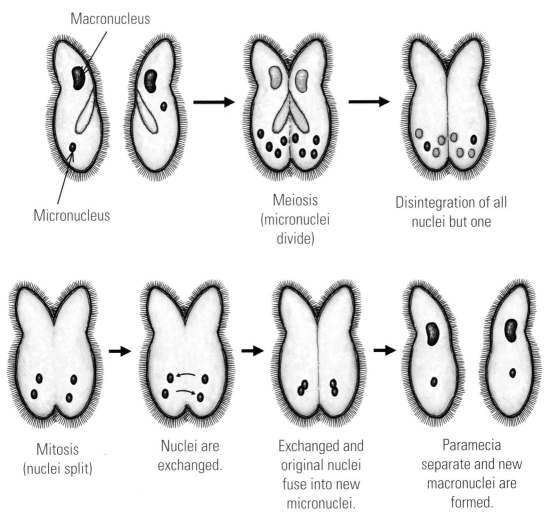

Macronucleus

Micronucleus

Meiosis
(micronuclei
divide)

Disintegration of all
nuclei but one

Mitosis
(nuclei split)

Nuclei are
exchanged.

Exchanged and
original nuclei
fuse into new
micronuclei.

Paramecia
separate and new
macronuclei are
formed.

chapter 3

FUNgi Facts

Scientists believe there are approximately 1.5 million different species of fungi, but only about 100,000 of these have been identified. Mushrooms, molds, mildews, and yeasts are fungi that may sound familiar to you.

Scientists of Significance

Pier Antonio Micheli (1679–1737) was an Italian botanist who worked as a professor at the University of Pisa and served as the director of the Botanical Garden of Florence. Micheli is considered the founder of **mycology**, the study of fungi. His scientific studies showed that mushrooms and molds grow from **spores** instead of spontaneously generating as previously believed. In his book *Nova plantarum generum*, Micheli described numerous plants and fungi. The book was a major advancement in scientific knowledge of fungi.

Robert H. Whittaker (1920–1980) was an American vegetation ecologist well known for his analysis of plant community ecology. Since the days of Micheli, fungi had been considered a subcategory of plants, not a separate group. In 1969, Whittaker successfully initiated an effort to change the classification system to include a separate kingdom for fungi.

Body Basics

Fungal bodies range from microscopic to gigantic. Unicellular microsporidia are as small as 1 micrometer. A giant multicellular fungus called *Armillaria ostoyae*, on the other hand, is estimated to spread across 2200 acres in the Malheur National Forest of eastern Oregon. Interestingly, neither of these fungi is seen often—at least not completely. Why? The first is just too tiny to see without a microscope. The second is primarily located underground. The only parts visible aboveground are the **fruiting bodies** known as mushrooms.

These mushrooms are part of a large growth of *Armillaria ostoyae* found in the Swiss National Park in Europe.

19

Fungi may be unicellular or multicellular, but the majority of them are multicellular. These multicellular bodies are made up of **hyphae**. Hyphae are cellular filaments (strands). These filaments are covered by a flexible cell wall of **chitin**, the same material that makes up the outer shells of insects and crustaceans.

The interwoven meshwork formed by the hyphae is called a **mycelium.** This body design maximizes the surface area exposed to the environment, increasing the absorption of nutrients and water. Since they lack structures for movement, fungi rely on mycelial growth to reach food sources.

Fungus Structure

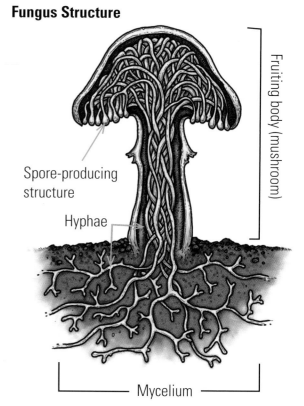

Spore-producing structure

Hyphae

Fruiting body (mushroom)

Mycelium

Fungal Hunter

Arthrobotrys, a soil fungus, is one of a small number of fungi that are considered carnivorous (meat-eating). These fungi use special hyphae to lasso and inject roundworms with digestive enzymes.

Time to Eat!

All fungal life is considered heterotrophic, and the majority of them are decomposers. Fungal decomposers are also known as **saprobes**. Digestion in saprobes occurs externally. These organisms secrete powerful enzymes onto a food source to break it down into smaller molecules that can be easily absorbed across the surface of the hyphae.

Fungal Lifestyles

The majority of fungi are free-living. Fungi that *do* form symbiotic relationships usually absorb simple organic molecules from their hosts. Some of these relationships are beneficial to the host and others are not.

Mycorrhizae

Mycorrhizae (meye kuh REYE zee) are mutualistic relationships between fungi and the roots of plants. The fungi give the plants water and vital minerals, and the plants give the fungi the sugar they need. About 95 percent of all plants maintain this type of relationship with fungi.

Mycorrhizae
(root and hyphae
together)

Tree root

Fungal hyphae

Lichens

Lichens (LEYE kuhns) are mutualistic relationships between fungi and bacterial blue-green algae or green algae. The fungi benefit by absorbing nutrients directly from the algae. The algae benefit by getting a safe habitat, water, and inorganic nutrients from the fungi. This relationship also allows both organisms to exist in a wider range of environments.

Lichen Structure

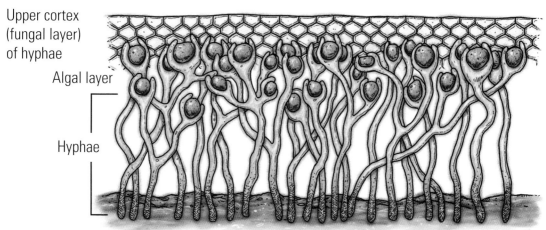

Upper cortex (fungal layer) of hyphae

Algal layer

Hyphae

Rock surface

Molds and Mildews

Molds are saprobes or parasites that grow on the surface of objects made from or inhabited by organic matter. They tend to appear as fuzzy layers on top of the object. Mildews are molds that tend to grow in very wet environments such as bathrooms and kitchens but can be found anywhere. They normally appear grayish in color and are more powdery than other molds.

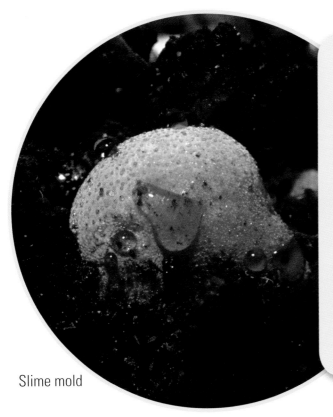

Slime mold

Do Not Make a Moldy Mistake!

Although they share the same name and certain characteristics, water and slime molds are *not* fungi. While these two "molds" are usually decomposers like fungi, they can move by themselves and their cellular structure is different from that of fungi. Therefore, they are classified as protists, not fungi.

Yeasts

Yeasts are unicellular fungi that can function as decomposers or parasites. In some cases, they can change from one to the other when needed. Yeasts are often found in environments with little oxygen because they can produce energy without the use of oxygen. This process is called *fermentation*.

A yeast called *Saccharomyces cerevisiae* is used in bread doughs to make them rise.

Inquire and Investigate: Yeast Fuel

Question

Is oil or sugar a better energy source for yeast fermentation?

Answer the Question

I think _____ is a better energy source for yeast fermentation.

Form a Hypothesis

(Oil/Sugar) is a better energy source for yeast fermentation.

Test the Hypothesis

Materials

- 3 clean plastic 20-oz. pop or water bottles and lids
- permanent marker
- liquid measuring cup
- water
- 1 package of dry fast-rising baker's yeast
- measuring spoons
- ¼ teaspoon of salt
- mixing bowl
- spoon
- funnel
- 2 tablespoons of cooking oil
- 2 tablespoons of granulated sugar (sucrose)
- 3 balloons (big enough to fit over bottle tops)

Procedure

1. Label the bottles 1, 2, and 3.
2. Mix 2¾ cups warm water, the yeast, and the salt in the bowl. Let stand for about 10 minutes.
3. Stir the yeast solution again. Use the funnel to pour equal amounts of the yeast mixture into the three bottles.
4. Add 2 tablespoons of water to bottle #1. (This is your control.)
5. Add 2 tablespoons of oil to bottle #2.
6. Add 2 tablespoons of sugar to bottle #3.
7. Put the lid on each bottle, and shake vigorously for 30 seconds.
8. Working with one bottle at a time, remove the lid and stretch the mouth of the balloon over the top of the bottle.
9. Check the bottles/balloons every 20 minutes for 2 hours. Record your observations. After each observation, swish the bottles carefully to maintain the distribution of the yeast.

Observations

Bottle #1 shows little or no change in the volume of the balloon. Bottle #2 shows little or no volume change. Bottle #3 shows the greatest change in volume.

Conclusions

Sugar is a better energy source for yeast fermentation. The fermentation of sugar by yeast produces energy for the yeast along with carbon dioxide gas and ethanol. The release of the carbon dioxide gas inflated the balloon on bottle #3.

Home Is Where the Habitat Is

Fungi are found in moist environments everywhere. Woods and grassy meadows are ideal for fungi that depend on plant roots, soil, and rotting wood and leaves. Front and back yards in rainy climates work just as well for these moisture-loving saprobes.

Yeasts and molds love damp places where organic matter can be found. This is why they inhabit spoiling food or bathroom surfaces that have a moist film of microscopic organisms on them.

Aquatic fungi, such as molds, live in ponds, streams, and other bodies of water. Their reproductive spores can travel by water instead of relying on air or other methods.

Lichens are often found growing on rocks. They can even exist in colder or drier environments where other living things may be threatened.

Shelf fungi on a tree

Lichens on a rock

The Cycle of Life

Like protists, fungi can reproduce either sexually, asexually, or both ways. In the case of unicellular fungi, reproduction tends to be asexual by binary fission or by budding. Yeasts, for example, can reproduce by growing new cells, or buds, and then pinching them off to form new organisms.

Multicellular fungi normally develop sexual and/or asexual organs that produce spores. Spores are inactive reproductive cells that are spread by wind, water, or animals. When they land in an ideal setting, they will sprout into new offspring.

Budding yeast

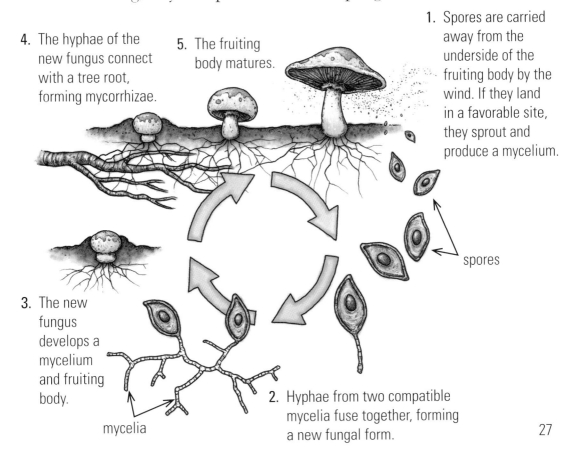

4. The hyphae of the new fungus connect with a tree root, forming mycorrhizae.

5. The fruiting body matures.

1. Spores are carried away from the underside of the fruiting body by the wind. If they land in a favorable site, they sprout and produce a mycelium.

spores

3. The new fungus develops a mycelium and fruiting body.

mycelia

2. Hyphae from two compatible mycelia fuse together, forming a new fungal form.

27

Club fungi produce spores sexually in large aboveground structures called *fruiting bodies*. These fruiting bodies are more commonly known as mushrooms. A single mushroom can disperse up to a billion spores into the air. The rest of the fungus stays hidden underground.

Sac fungi also produce spores in fruiting bodies. Some of these fungi produce fruiting bodies that lie below the surface, while others extend aboveground. Truffles are the underground fruiting bodies of certain sac fungi. Morel mushrooms are aboveground fruiting bodies of other types of sac fungi.

Truffles

Morel mushrooms

chapter 4

The Positives and Negatives of Protists and Fungi

You might think of protists and fungi as just seaweed and mushrooms, but in reality, both of these groups of organisms affect your everyday life in big and small ways. Many of these effects are beneficial, while a few can be harmful.

The Positives
Protist and Fungi Products

Algae has many uses. The Japanese use seaweeds in soups, dried snacks, and sushi wraps. Kelp is used as a mulch or fertilizer for crops. Thickening agents are extracted from brown and red algae and used in many food products such as soups and ice creams. One of these agents, agar, is also used to grow specimens in research laboratories.

Baker's yeast plays an important role in the rising of bread products. Alcohol production also depends on yeast fermentation.

Molds are used to make certain antibiotics that fight bacterial infections. Penicillin is one of these mold-based medicines. Molds are also used in food products such as soy sauce and cheese.

The farming, harvesting, and selling of mushrooms, truffles, and morels is a big business. People love to hunt for and eat these fungal delights.

Ecosystem Effects

Algae play a key role in their own **ecosystems** as well as the global ecosystem. As a producer, algae form the first link in many food chains. Because of their vast numbers, they supply almost half of the Earth's oxygen during photosynthesis. Sometimes algae form their own ecosystems. The kelp forest of Monterey Bay, for instance, serves as a meal for some, a hunting ground for others, and a home for many.

In order for an ecosystem to survive, those that die must be recycled. The fungal saprobes make sure this happens. Without them, dead matter would accumulate and inorganic nutrients would run out.

In addition to recycling, some fungi can clean up the environment as well. Scientists are now using certain fungi, along with some protists, to absorb toxic chemicals in soil and water and neutralize or decompose them into less harmful substances. This process is called *bioremediation*.

Kelp forest along the California coast

The mutualistic relationships of fungi and protists benefit more than just the partners. They also benefit the whole community. For example, without the formation of mycorrhizae, it would be very difficult for plants in a forest to absorb adequate water and minerals. Since these plants serve as food and shelter, without them, the rest of the community would begin to disappear.

Coral reefs are another example. Coral reefs are the remains of tiny animals called *coral polyps*. Algae called *zooanthellae* live in these polyps, providing them with carbohydrates they need. When environmental factors such as global warming or pollution cause the algae to die or leave the coral host, the polyps die as well. This is known as coral bleaching. Coral reefs can be home to millions of organisms. When the reefs disappear, so do the organisms.

Coral reefs

Algal bloom on a reservoir in England

The Negatives
An Overabundance of Algae

You might think that since algae are so helpful, the more the better. Not necessarily. A sudden surge in algae population is called an *algal bloom*. These blooms usually end up being detrimental to an ecosystem. As quickly as the algae bloom, they die back. This causes major decomposition that uses up excessive amounts of oxygen in the water. This leads to the suffocation and death of aquatic life.

A red tide is an algal bloom of certain dinoflagellates that turns the nearby coastline red. Some of these dinoflagellates produce toxins that harm or kill aquatic wildlife and the animals that feed on them. It is believed that global warming and certain pollutants may be increasing the presence and severity of these activities.

33

Technology Link

Advancements in technology have improved the prediction and tracking of red tides. The monitoring of water temperatures, oxygen levels, toxin levels, and specific algae presence can now be done using sensors in remote, automated, in-water laboratories. One type of sensor detects algal  blooms by comparing light passing through seawater with and without algae. Water with algae in it will contain a pigment that affects the passage of light through it. Satellites are used to send these and other test results directly to scientists moments after the samples are taken. This, along with satellite photos, helps scientists locate and respond to algal bloom hotspots.

Infected!

Several common infections are caused by fungi. The infection caused by *Candida albicans* is commonly known as a yeast infection, thrush, or diaper rash, depending on where it occurs on the body. These infections are normally not dangerous but can be annoying if left untreated. Fungi are also responsible for the itchy rash between toes commonly called *athlete's foot*. Warm, sweaty shoes create a perfect environment for the growth of these fungi.

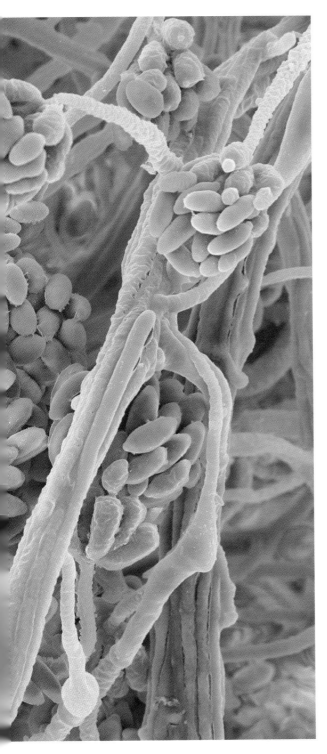

Poisonous Protists and Fungi

Marine algae known as dinoflagellates contain and/or release toxins. When humans consume seafoods that have accumulated these poisons, the results can be fatal.

Some fungi produce chemicals called **mycotoxins** that can be dangerous to those who come in contact with them. In the past, black mold has stirred up a lot of discussion. This mold thrives in homes that have continual moisture problems. Even though it has yet to be proven, many believe that the mold has caused serious health problems for those who have been exposed to its spores.

Another mycotoxin of concern is aflatoxin. Secreted by the *Aspergillus* fungus, this toxin can grow on improperly stored grain. Aflatoxin is known to cause certain kinds of cancer.

Stachybotrys chartarum is a slimy black mold that produces mycotoxins that are poisonous when inhaled. The mold grows on moist paper, sheet rock, and other materials containing cellulose.

Crop Concerns

Approximately 70 percent of crop diseases are caused by fungi or fungilike protists. Corn smut is a fungal parasite that infects ears of corn. This disease is rarely widespread and causes little more than an annoyance for a farmer. Fungal rust, on the other hand, is very infectious and can cause a dramatic reduction in crop yield.

The protist *Phytopthora infestans* is responsible for the potato blight (disease) that caused the Great Potato Famine in Ireland more than 150 years ago. Because this protist is still a major concern to potato growers all over the world, scientists have been working on developing blight-resistant potato species.

Corn smut

Protists and fungi may seem small and unimportant at first glance, but don't be fooled. These organisms have some pivotal roles in our daily lives and our ecosystems. So stay on the lookout for these diverse organisms!

http://biology4kids.com/files/micro_protozoa.html
Biology4kids presents interesting information on protozoa, fungi, and lichens.

http://www.microbe.org/microbes/what_is.asp
Unravel the mysteries of protists and fungi by clicking on their links at this site.

http://herbarium.usu.edu/fungi/FunFacts/factindx.htm
Learn more fun facts about fungi, and then apply them to the experiments, puzzles, and games found here.

http://www.doctorfungus.org/thefungi/index.htm
"Doctor Fungus" introduces you to the world of fungi.

http://mgd.nacse.org/hyperSQL/lichenland/html/biology/meeting.html
See what happens when Mr. Fungi meets an Alga and creates the Lichen with this information and diagrams.

algae (AL jee) plantlike group of protists that carry out photosynthesis; plural of *alga*

amoeba (uh MEE buh) protist that uses extensions called *pseudopodia* to produce an "oozing" movement

chitin (KEYE tuhn) material that makes up the hard outer covering on fungi and other organisms

ciliate (SIL ee uht) protist that moves by means of short extensions called *cilia*

dormant (DOR muhnt) temporarily inactive

ecosystem (EEK oh sis tuhm) group of organisms and the environment they live in

endocytosis (end oh seye TOH sis) the engulfing of nutrients by a cell

flagellate (FLAJ uh luht) protist that moves by means of long extensions called *flagellum*

fruiting body (FROO ting BAH dee) part of some fungi from which spores are released

fungi (FUHNG eye) organisms that live by absorbing nutrients from other organisms; plural of *fungus*

heterotroph (HET uh ruh trohf) organism that gets its food by consuming other organisms or their by-products

hyphae (HEYE fee) filaments, or strands, that make up the body of a fungus

mycelium (meye SEE lee uhm) mass of hyphae that forms the body of a fungus

mycology (meye KAHL uh jee) scientific study of fungi

mycotoxin (MEYE koh tahk sin) poisonous chemical produced by fungi

phagocytosis (fay goh seye TOH sis) the engulfing of large molecules or cells by a cell

photoautotroph (foh toh AW tuh trohf) organism that produces its own food through the process of photosynthesis

protist (PROH tist) eukaryote organism that is neither plant, animal, nor fungus

protozoan (proh tuh ZOH uhn) heterotrophic protist that moves by itself

saprobe (SAP rohb) organism that gets nutrients from nonliving organic matter; decomposer

spore (spor) small reproductive structure that's capable of developing into a new individual

symbiosis (sim bee OH sis) close relationship between two different types of organisms